Copyright @ Dr P. J. Kennedy 2018
Edited and Illustrated by Anne Curtis

All rights reserved. You may not copy, store, distribute, transmit, reproduce or otherwise make available this publication (or any part of it) in any form, or by any means (electronic, digital, optical, mechanical, photocopying, recording or otherwise), without the prior written permission of the publisher.

for my daughter who shines her light every day xoxxoxx

Contents

Lucia and the Wired Brain · 4

Lucia and the Optometrist · 16

Lucia and the Tooth Fairy · 26

Lucia and Big Ben · 36

Lucia and the Pool Handstand · 46

Lucia and the Wired Brain

By P. J. Kennedy and Anne Curtis

Lucia IS a delightful wee child
Who can light up the world with her twinkling eye,
And her beaming white smile
and her cute little nose,
(She often tickles her daddy when he's in repose).

A fantabulous Friday,
a weekend for action,
'Get straight to your bed it is time for chillaxin'
Said Lucia's Daddy, 'But I'm not really tired,
My body wants sleep but my brain is still wired!'

'Really?' said Daddy, as they walked up the stair,
'Let's see when you're bathed,
(take a brush for your hair),
We will get you all snuggled,
then a story or two,
And if you're still wired, I'll count dolphins for you!'

'Ok,' said Lucia in her bedtime pyjamas,
'But could you count elephants
eating bananas?
Please, double please
would you do this for me?
There's lots of bananas need eating you see!'

'If you're still awake, off course I'll do that,
I am happy to help you and that is a fact.'
They made with their pinkies, a promise to keep,
Once daddy had finished, Lucia would sleep.

So stories were read,
(it was three for good luck),
Then her Daddy spent time,
Tucking Lucia up.
He turned Lucia's pillow,
she liked it that way,
All snuggly and warm...
in a cuddly way.

So counting the dolphins began: 1 – 2 – 3,
100 blue dolphins in a dream-filled sea!
And sleepy filled eyes gently closed to dream on,
To find where the lovely blue dolphins had gone.

Daddy took a step back
and looked tenderly down
On his beautiful child
all cosey and sound.

She had fallen asleep
and straight into her dream,
Her body and brain were now tired
it would seem.

It was time for her Daddy to start to unwind,
To tidy the kitchen,
relax and recline.
'Nobody knows what tomorrow will bring,'
He thought
' an adventure might make her heart sing'.

'But there's one thing for sure
and I certainly know
That Lucia will be bursting to run to and fro!
To learn to her best,
come wind and come rain
Till her body and brain
need relaxing again!'

'Dream beautiful dreams my dearest sweetheart
And I'll clean pots and pans with you deep in my heart.'
That evening her Daddy put up both of his feet,

'Lights out, it's now time for my own comfy sleep!'

The table was set, all ordered and neat,
Scrambled eggs and white toast, for breakfast-y treat!
'The food for adventures!' Lucia will boast
'There's nothing my Wired Brain loves more than some toast!'

Thank you Daddy!

The End

Lucia
and
The Optometrist
By P. J. Kennedy and Anne Curtis

Lucia IS a delightful wee child
Who can light up the world with her twinkling eye,
And her beaming white smile
and her cute little nose,
(She often tickles her daddy when he's in repose).

A fantabulous Saturday ...and first on the list
Was to visit a very smart optometrist.
So into the car and a drive into town,
With Lucia in charge of her daddy's iPhone.
(Blasting out her favourite songs!)

They arrived at 10.30,
not a moment too soon,
And both took a seat in the small waiting room.
The optometrist's name,
they both knew as Billy
They'd heard he was strange
and they'd heard he was silly!
But at checking your eyes he was surely the best,
And before very long he'd be put to the test!

'I am going to test how you see near and far,
In the light and the dark,
so just stay as you are,
But don't fall asleep as I need you alert,
Eyes open Lucia,
you'll find it wont hurt.'

She smiled at her daddy who was patiently waiting,
He gave her 'thumbs up' without hesitating,
I can see 1, 2, 3, A, B C ...that was easy!
But the animal shapes make me feel quite uneasy.
They're all fuzzy and wobbly,
I can't make them out.
'I can help you Lucia, of that there's no doubt.'

'Now,' whispered Billy. 'You are doing just fine,
Let's try on these glasses and just take your time
To look at the screen and repeat every letter.
With these magical glasses you'll see so much better!'

Then he dropped in some lenses, 'Oh My!' cried Lucia,
Then she named all the animals, distant and nearer.
Counted right up to ten, said the alphabet too!
'These glasses are perfect — I think these will do!'

'Your eyes are just fine, but a little prescription,
Will undoubtedly help with improving your vision.
You can choose some nice frames
with some help from your Daddy,
Then in a week's time your glasses will be ready.'

Lucia stared very hard,
she could see crystal clear,
She was wearing pink glasses
in sparkling veneer.
These are just perfect!
You're magical Billy,
You're ever so clever
and not at all silly!'

So seven days later they returned to see Billy,
(Whoever had said he's inclined to be silly?)
She tried on her glasses,
a perfect neat fit.
'One moment,' said Billy as he polished a bit...

'There!'

Lucia was smiling, Her heart feeling lighter,
'Oh Daddy!
With my magic pink glasses, the world's so much brighter!'

The End

Lucia and The Tooth Fairy

By P. J. Kennedy and Anne Curtis

Lucia IS a delightful wee child
Who can light up the world with her twinkling eye,
And her beaming white smile
and her cute little nose,
(She often tickles her daddy when he's in repose).

One glorious Sunday when Lucia woke,
She gave her front tooth a gentle wee poke.
'Daddy – it's loose!' (Of that there's no doubt)
'Will the tooth fairy visit and help it fall out?'

'Perhaps,' said her Dad as she opened her mouth,
And there hung her tooth like a wobbly old trout!
'Hmmm – better not touch it,
just leave well alone,
I'm sure it will fall out in time, on its own!'

And the very next day, not long before noon,
FLOP went the tooth...
straight onto her spoon!
'It's out! It's out!' little Lucia exclaimed,
(Relieved that the rest of her teeth still remained!)

So under her pillow she popped it that night
I'll stay here and wish the tooth fairy goodnight.
But Lucia was far too excited to sleep,
What if she met her...Madame Coochy-Peep?
(For she was the fairy so secret and wise
Who replaced fallen teeth with a lovely surprise!)

That night as she slept
she had beautiful dreams
Of wonder and fairies from magical realms.
And then as she dreamt Madame Coochy-Peep came,
From her home in the garden – the fairies' domain.
Her wings were like jewels.
She hummed a sweet tune,
Sprinkling magical dust around Lucia's room.

And there was a tooth (much to her delight) –
' Neath Lucia's pillow – so clean and so bright!
' I'll leave her a prize as her tooth is so clean
She needs a reward so she'll know that I've been.'

In the blink of an eye
Madame Coochy-Peep spread
Invisible dust around Lucia's head.
To make it all work
for this is a must,
A sprinkle of powdery, fairy-like -dust.

When Lucia woke she sat straight up in bed
And wondered at dreams going round in her head.
She lifted her pillow with sleepy filled eyes,
Peeked just underneath, could there be a surprise?

"OH!"

'Daddy – she's been in the middle of night,
To leave me a coin so golden and bright!
I'll take it to school so as others will know,
If you care for you teeth then the richer you'll grow!'

(And further to that if you don't clean your teeth
There'll be no reward from Madame Coochy-Peep!

(...Or she may leave you an crumbly old leaf...
or something ha ha!)

The End

Lucia and BIG BEN
By P. J. Kennedy and Anne Curtis

Lucia IS a delightful wee child
Who can light up the world with her twinkling eye,
And her beaming white smile
and her cute little nose,
(She often tickles her daddy when he's in repose).

It was early Monday morning when daddy and Lucia
Travelled up to London for another great adventure.

The date would be auspicious,
but Lucia wouldn't know,
BIG BEN was in BIG trouble,
but of course it didn't show.

The crowd stood next to Winston,
looking up and looking down.
Expectantly awaiting,
London City's famous sound.

But on the 21st August,
the year 2017,
BIG BEN fell still and silent,
in a state of quarantine.
At 12 o'clock mid-day he chimed one BIG almighty

bong!

An 'E' rang out so loud and clear,
the last note of his song.

"At least for 4 long years or more
BIG BEN will never speak,"
"But daddy, that is far too long,
I cannot wait a week!
And why has Big Ben stopped right now?
And why's he lost his voice?"
"I'm sad to say Big Ben is old.
There is no other choice."

You see he's really VERY old, (157 to be exact),
And for all those years BIG BEN's been there
and now it seems he's whacked!
Big Ben will wait in London Town, his hands still on his face,
Until his bell of 13 tonne will once more keep the pace.

"So please don't worry now, my child,
BIG BEN has been prepared,
For years of renovation whilst his workings are repaired.
Its only temporary (though he's in a poorly state),
Attention of the experts' sure to fix him,
just you wait!"

Eeee

But now he needs the Nation's love. We all must stand as one,
BIG BEN will chime and call the time for many years to come.
Till then he'll speak out twice a year and call the New Year in,
And on Remembrance Sunday, he will test his voice again.

And with each chime and sound of bell,
to everyone he'll call,
"Remember those who fought and died,
who sacrificed their all."
"He's certainly an icon,
standing up for what is right."
Said Lucia,
"He MUST speak again, I hope he'll be alright."

So here's to 2021, or perhaps it may be more?
We must be very patient if we want to hear him roar.
This Tower of strength will chime again and sing to this proud land,
Of justice, peace and freedom so with BIG BEN —
Let us stand (hand in hand!)

The End

Lucia and the Pool Handstand

By P. J. Kennedy and Anne Curtis

Lucia IS a delightful wee child
Who can light up the world with her twinkling eye,
And her beaming white smile
and her cute little nose,
(She often tickles her daddy when he's in repose).

A remarkable summer vacation
Full of play and exploration!
When by the pool Lucia
Had a wonderful idea!

All day long Lucia had been splishing in the pool,
And a-sploshing and a-splashing, and her friends had too.
Lucia had been trying to and dying to handstand,
She'd been practicing and practicing (though mainly on the land).

Her gliding was subliminal, her swimming just divine,
But a handstand was her aim and she'd decided it was time.
Lucia had been trying to and dying to handstand,
And to walk under the water not on feet but on her hands!

50

'That's fine by me,' said Daddy, 'If your ready, off you go
But the secret of this action is to listen, not to know.
So give me all your focus, your attention and your ears.
If you do not listen hard then you'll be practicing for years!'

'Stand in the pool, be tall and proud, begin to bend your knees.
Use the bottom like a springboard but don't dive yet (if you please),
Bring your hands up to Namaste and keep bouncing up and down,
Then jump high up with your head down, aim directly for the ground.'

'With your head under the water you will find you're upside down,
But once you reach the bottom hold your hands flat on the ground.
Remember to breathe out not in, it's not like on the land,
Just gently blow out bubbles through your watery handstand.'

'Then hold onto to the floor
with both your legs up in the air.
For now, you are hand-standing,
never thinking you'd be there!

Lucia was determined
and so soon she learnt the skill
Of hand-standing underwater
and it really was a thrill!'

The thrill was so delightful she decided to do more,
And a hundred handstands later she completely lost the score!
(But her Daddy hadn't... it was 134)

(...plus one more just for luck!)

135

The End

Printed in Great Britain
by Amazon